Archempress's Daughter 2

Ryan Stoute

A parade of rotating haloes plagued the skies outside of the classroom windows where Princess Seaphoenix Spoongold reviewed her college mathematics course problems.

Professor Dark Angles scribbled an ocean of equations across the board, which baffled his 26 students.

Several students, who sat near the royal, chattered about the ever increasing amount of swirling blobs smeared into a vast canvass of brilliant indigo.

Then, Spoongold also eyed the rampant zoo of meteorological beasts.

Wind gust speeds intensified and the brick facade crumbled.

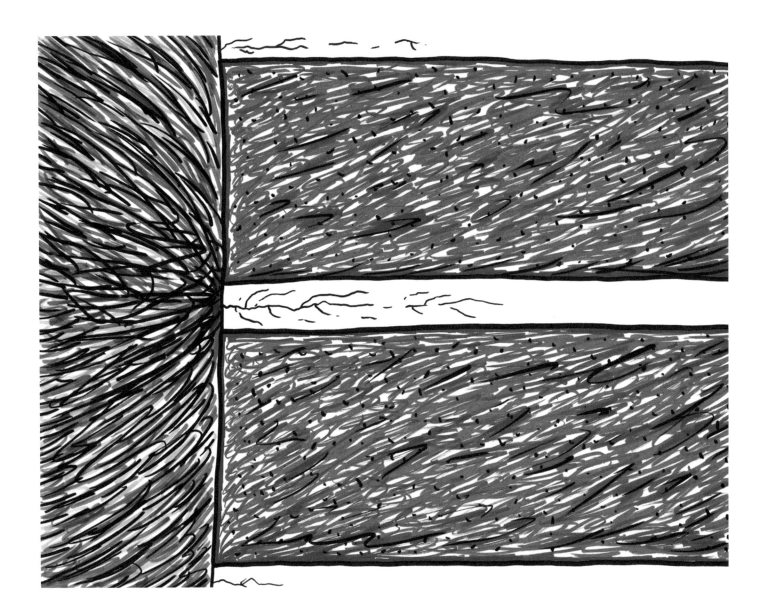

The invisible scorpionesque stings engulfed the instructor's lower neck. Distraught by this series of unfortunate discomforts, he wandered over to the windows and slammed them shut.

Resuming his aimless streaks of splintered chalk, his hairs were rattled by pulverized thrusts of tightened swirls, which pummeled the fragile panels of imported glass.

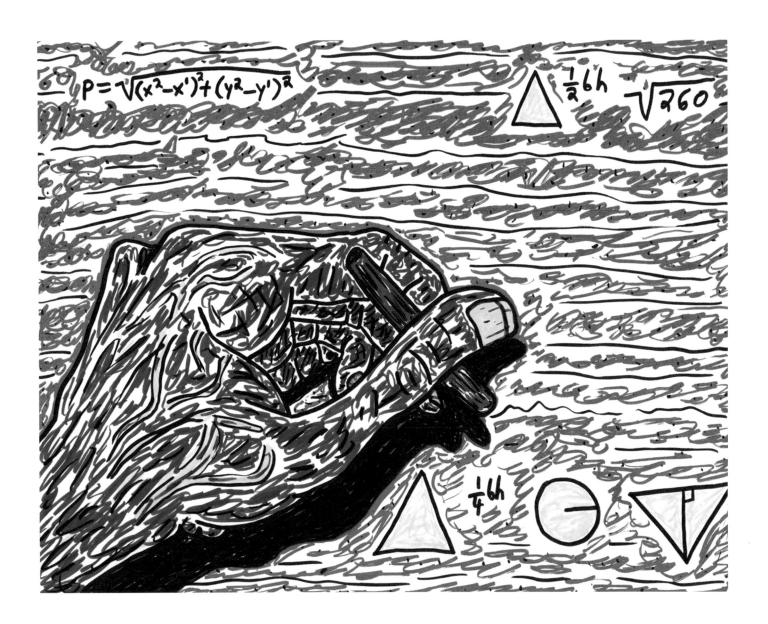

Eventually, there were more cracks in the windows' surfaces than the number of grains of sand on one of the planet's 674 million beaches.

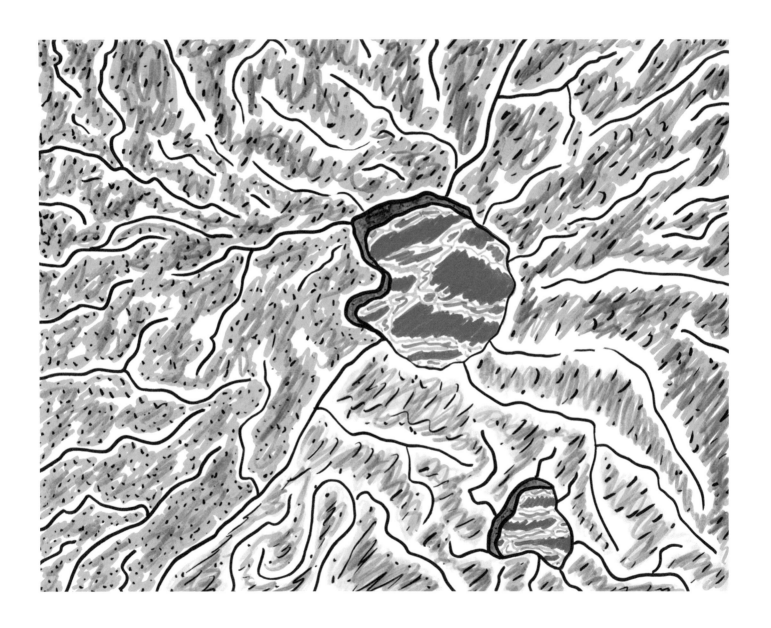

The teacher's forehead swam in a sea of cold sweat. His heart rate elevated to an alarming level; and an electrical pulse gyrated down his fingers causing the slab of tree salt chalk to snap in half.

Not waiting to be dismissed by the college authorities, the disheartened students packed their bags and hurried off to find a safe spot to shelter.

Seeing the fear in their eyes, Professor Angles stopped the lecture and directed the 26 pupils to stay away from the mangled windows.

Seventeen men and women found sanctuary inside the classroom closet. Unfortunately, the other nine sought protection elsewhere, which the princess was one of them.

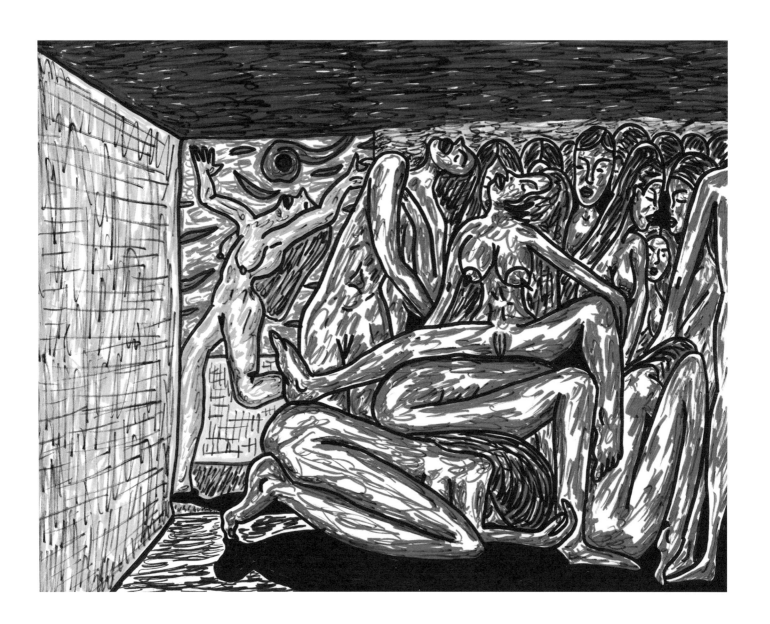

Outside the classroom door, Spoongold witnessed many millions of students, teachers, and other faculty scrambling to find places to hide throughout the college building's 470 million hallways located on Floor 26.

In a colorful sea of chaotic unison, moving bodies fluttered in one direction down a massive corridor.

The mindstaggering amount of people pouring out of the classrooms rose into the hundreds of billions; such that Princess Seaphoenix Spoongold lost sight of her eight classmates. Furthermore, a myriad of fallen persons were trampled to death under an endless procession of bare feet.

When the rattled royal realized all
the rooms were locked, blocked, or
filled to full capacity, she continued
her zigzagged path down the halls
of screaming hysteria.

Princess Spoongold, fatigued, held onto a locker and its door swung open. Immediately, she climbed inside and sealed the door shut with an interior lever. Releasing a long sigh, her lower face folded into a brief smile.

Shallow beacons of light silhouetted the locker's dark interior. Seaphoenix closed her eyes: She wondered what was happening? And the green-skinned woman questioned why out of the 444 quadrillion college-planets sprawled across this hyperspace-galaxy, she had chosen this one?

Seaphoenix's ears twitched at clanging metal and a staccato series of semi-perpetual shrieks. An avalanche of falls and collisions escalated. A carnival-procession of cold chills swam across the pretty princess's forehead. Peals of thunder cluttered, thuds shuttered, loud slaps sputtered, and pitch-sharp squeaks clattered. Spoongold's mind shivered into a frenetic frenzy of capsized diffusions.

Crouched down on the floor in a fetal position, the princess clutched her stomach, which flared into a fiery ocean of misfortunes.

The sound of millions of doors opening and closing in every direction irritated her eardrums.

Seaphoenix Spoongold lowered her head and grasped her knees. She rationalized whether this day would ever end?

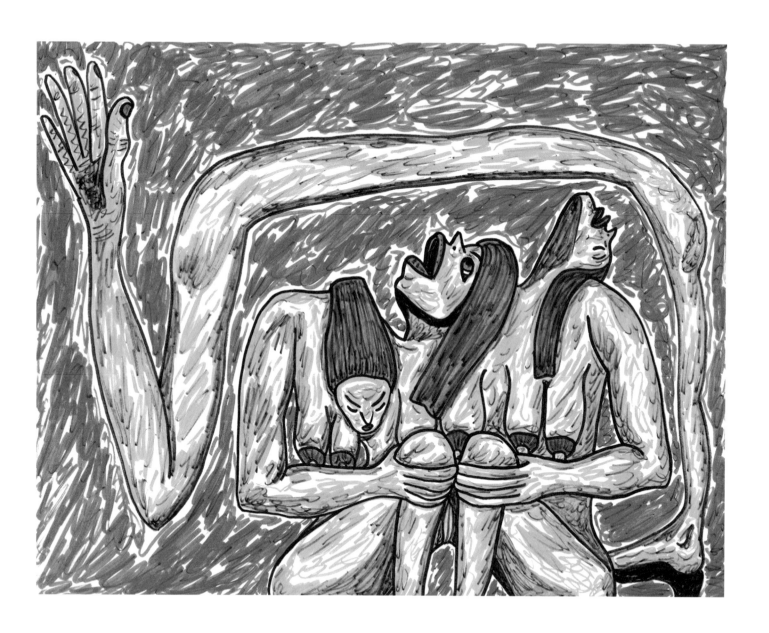

Wobbled screams and crushed footsteps of confusion bombarded outside her hidden chamber. Next, the princess's skin convulsed in a series of dense squeezes.

Twenty-eight seconds after the last convulsion, all sounds outside her locker dissipated.

The royal's hands were embalmed in an invisible layer of high energies. And her body became light as a leaf-feather.

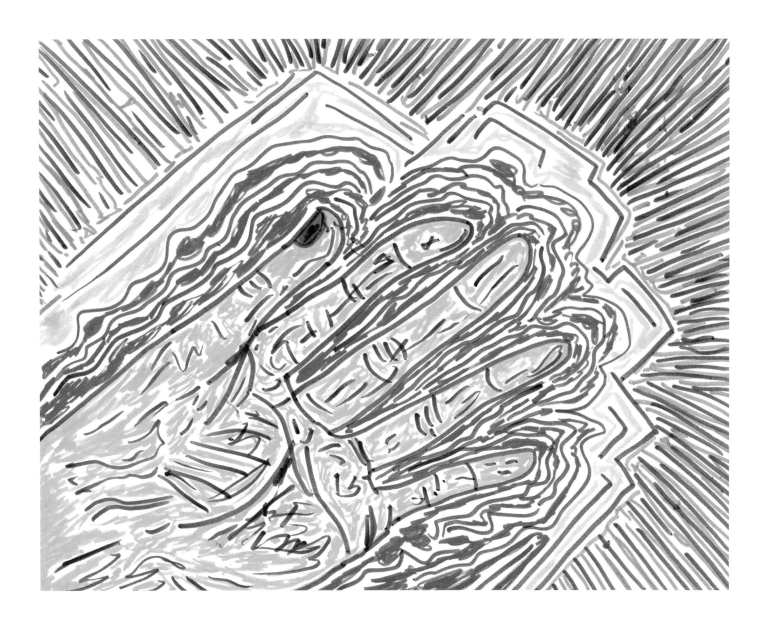

Becoming light-headed from these newly-acquired sensations, Spoongold closed her eyes to rest.

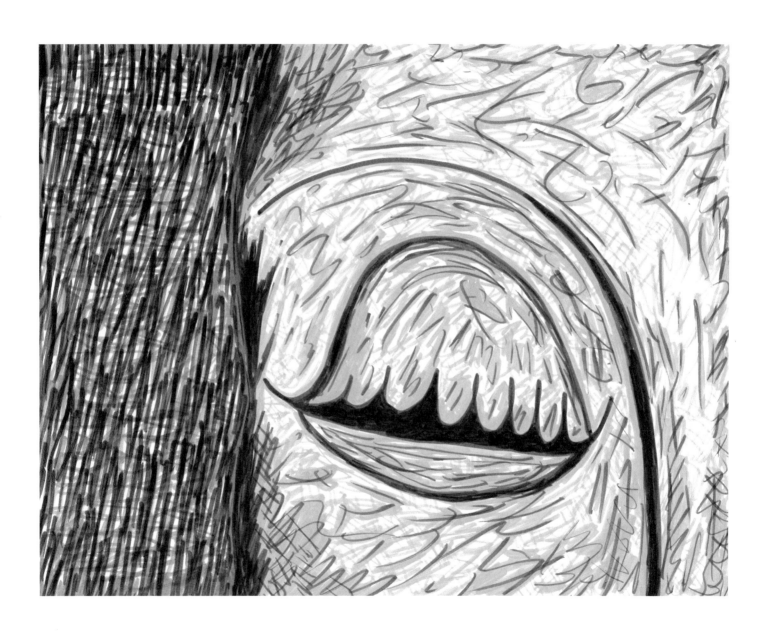

Minutes later, the bewildered princess unlocked the locker door and effortlessly glided like a thin piece of paper down to the liquid-covered floors. Moreover, it dawned on her that these floors had descended many stories below their original locations.

Countless billions of dead bodies bobbled inside a slime-infested sea made from quintillions of mitochondria-nodules. And the lifeless cadavers emitted an eerie iridescent golden glow.

Princess Seaphoenix's soles touched the odorless substance before the agile thrust from this quick motion lifted her whole body skyward.

Hovering, skyhopping, and gliding over large swaths of strange-yellow liquid, Spoongold landed on the phoenixchair where she wiped the enigmatic-adhesive off her feet and ankles.

After a five-hour wait on the elusive piece of furniture, the royal came to the conclusion that no one was coming to rescue her.

Inflated bodies floated everywhere and they decayed at an unusual speed.

This gelatinous sticky liquid was composed of two kinds of mitochondria-nodules: Clockwise and counterclockwise. Furthermore, the clockwise nodules were more numerous than their counterparts; however, the counterclockwise nodules rotated four times faster than the clockwise variety.

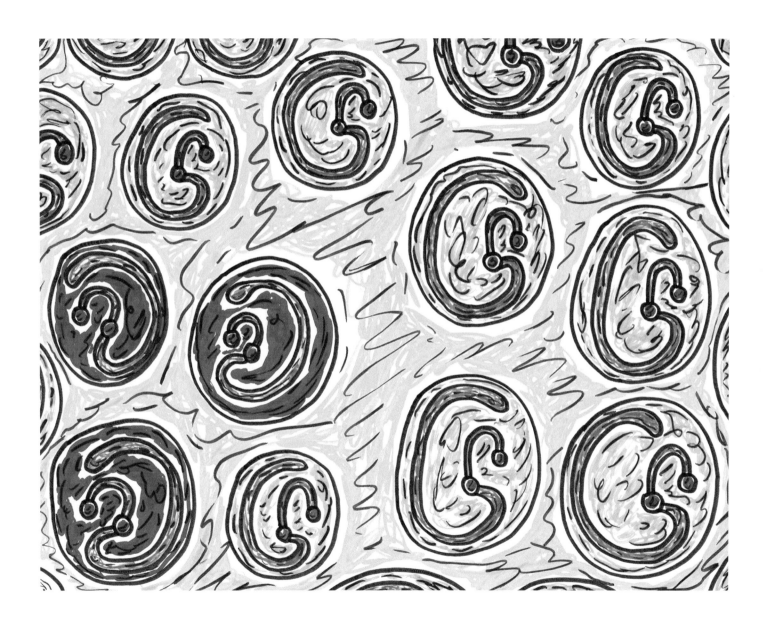

Therefore, due to the amazingly intricate complexity and interactions between these two types of nodules, billions of wandering remains disintegrated into a myriad of molecular chains, which swarmed and whirlpooled around each of the consuming mitochondria-nodules.

Whence, each devoured molecular string emitted a powerful flash of blue light equivalent to the brightness of an exploding 500-solar mass star.

And the indigo light also quickened the annihilation of the deceased.

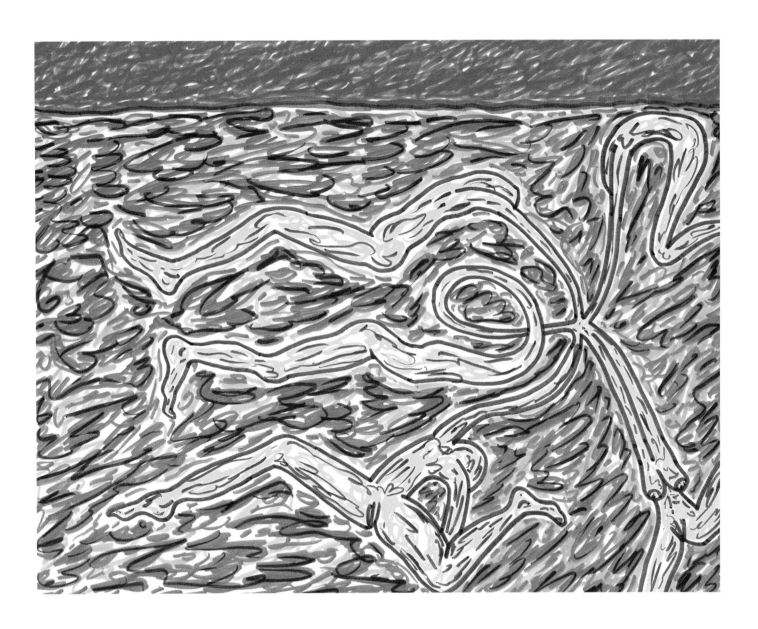

Forty-seven minutes later, all 952 billion corpses vanished inside the strange mitochondria creatures; and the slimy sauce chirped like a chorus of sea crickets.

The grimaced Princess Seaphoenix Spoongold laid in the chair startled as the chirps grew louder and the muck became concentrated into smaller pools of high density. When one of the pools reached optimal, an enormous hole carved its way across the floor, exposing the hallway on the level below. Next, the intrigued pretty princess leaped from the phoenixchair like a lioness and sat her feet on the ground.

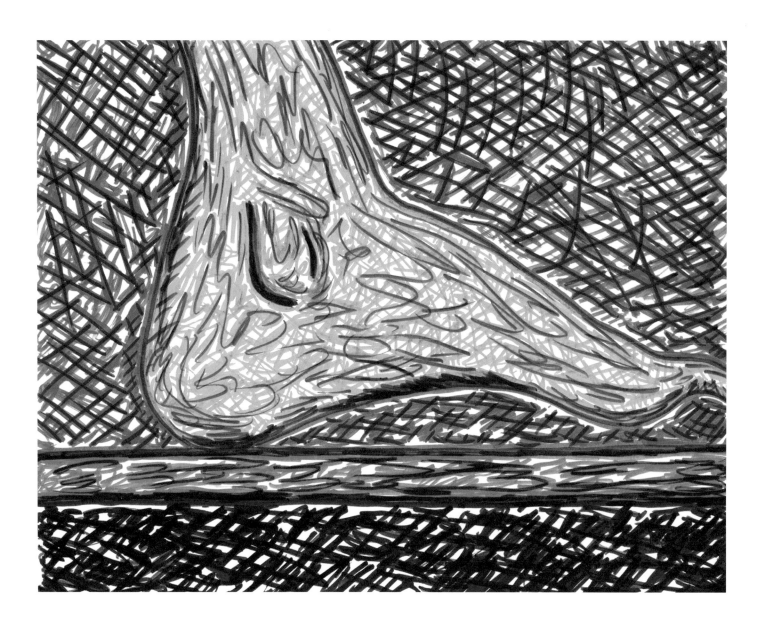

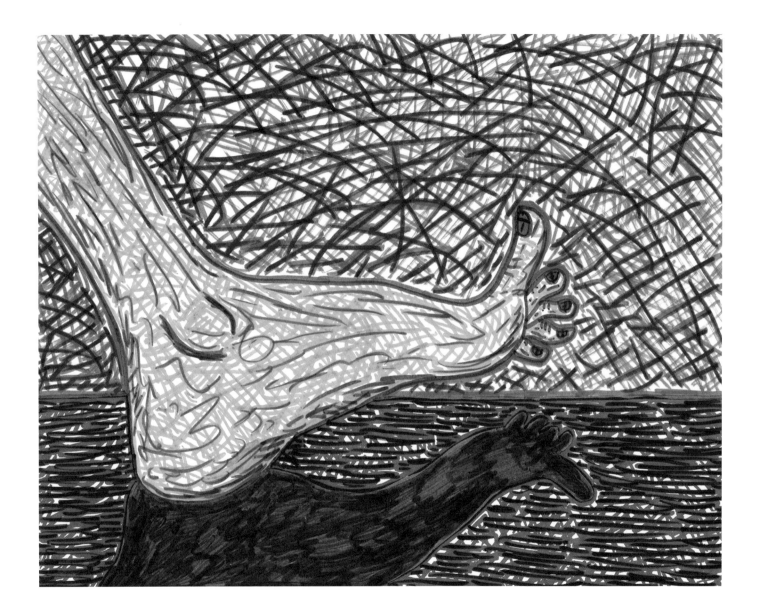

Invigorated with an anointed prowess, Spoongold dashed over to the gigantic hole in the floor and executed a triple front flip down to the next level.

Princess Seaphoenix searched the corridors for hours; then, as she was about to give up, a murky blur of yellow came into view.

It was an intrepid man named Snowmustard Railcurtain. The green-skinned female was smittened by his charmingly good looks; and they flirted with each other for seventeen minutes.

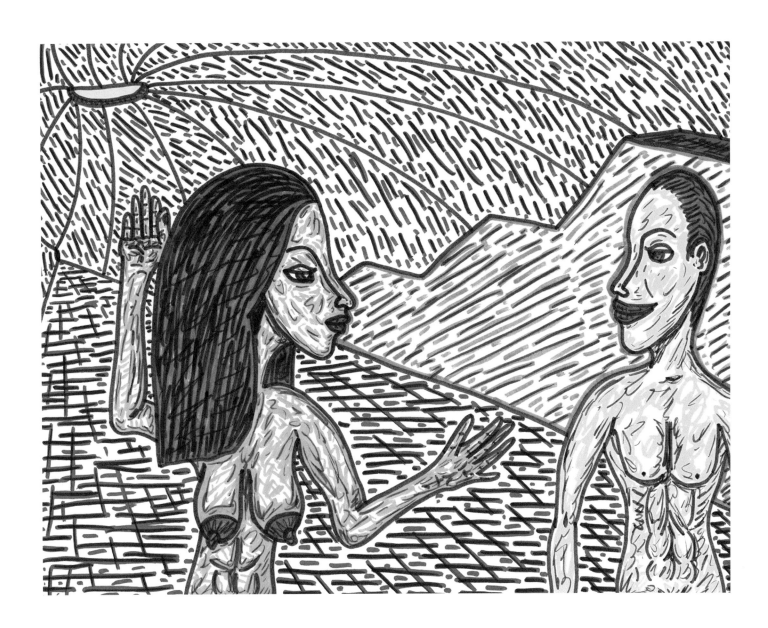

After a long witty session of chatting and laughter, he lifted up his hand and unfolded the fingers to expose the multiple orange circles. These mysterious protuberances were testicles and godspots.

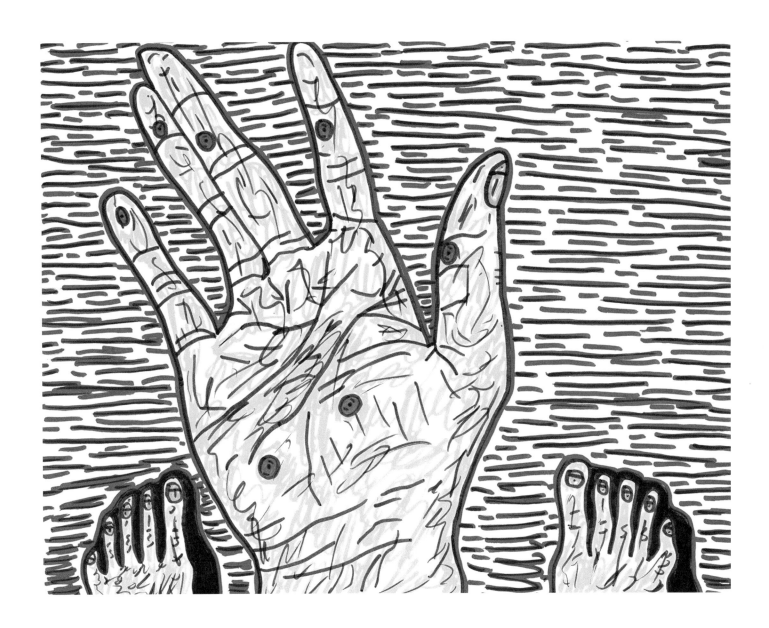

Spoongold raised her left foot up off the ground and placed it inside the palm of his hand; and he went in to her in such a manner.

Twenty-eight minutes after intercourse, a most beautiful turquoise-colored oval came out of her mouth. They marveled at this egg they had created together.

Gently laying the egg on the ground, the royal princess incubated the smooth and fragile creation underneath the warm flesh of her delicately-wrinkled left sole.

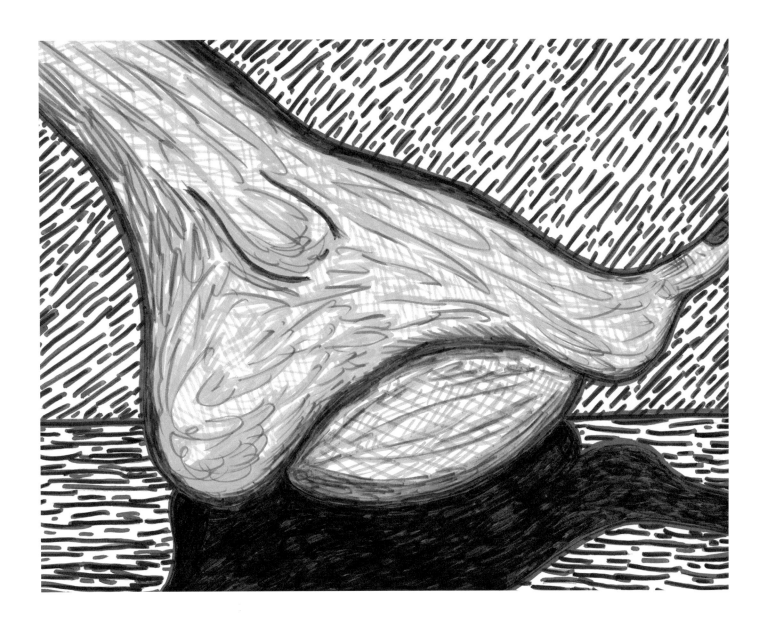

When the pristine elliptical egg obtained prime temperature, humidity and viscosity, the couple inserted themselves inside. Their bodies merged together and changed into a thick golden yolk with indistinguishable homogeneous features.

The unscathed oval nestled quietly on the floor for twenty-six days. And on the twenty-seventh day, an orange hand reached down to snatch it away to an undisclosed location.

Ryan Stoute currently lives in Chelsea, Massachusetts and is an author of twenty-eight full-color Trafford Publishing book titles. He earned degrees in English and in science at Bunker Hill Community College and the University of Massachusetts in Boston.

Order this book online at www.trafford.com
or email orders@trafford.com

Most Trafford titles are also available at major online book retailers.

 www.trafford.com

North America & international
toll-free: 844 688 6899 (USA & Canada)
fax: 812 355 4082

Our mission is to efficiently provide the world's finest, most comprehensive book publishing
service, enabling every author to experience success. To find out how to publish your book,
your way, and have it available worldwide, visit us online at www.trafford.com

ISBN: 978-1-6987-1336-6 (sc)

ISBN: 978-1-6987-1335-9 (e)

Library of Congress Control Number: 2022911090

Print information available on the last page.

Trafford rev.11/17/2022

Printed in the United States
by Baker & Taylor Publisher Services